If I Were a LION

For my Whistlepig pals, Tom and Dan
—S. W.
For Rennie, Hannah, and Zoë
—H. M. S.

Atheneum Books for Young Readers
An imprint of Simon & Schuster Children's Publishing Division
1230 Avenue of the Americas, New York, New York 10020
Text copyright © 2004 by Sarah Weeks
Illustrations copyright © 2004 by Heather M. Solomon
Book design by Polly Kanevsky
The text of this book is set in Carlton.
The illustrations are rendered in watercolor and gouache.
Manufactured in China

14 16 18 20 19 17 15 13
Library of Congress Cataloging-in-Publication Data
Weeks, Sarah.
If I were a lion / Sarah Weeks ; illustrated by Heather M. Solomon.—1st ed.
p.   cm.
Summary: A young girl imagines how wild she could be if she were an animal.
ISBN 978-0-689-84836-0
[1. Behavior—Fiction. 2. Imagination—Fiction. 3. Animals—Fiction. 4. Stories in rhyme.]
I. Solomon, Heather M. ill. II. Title.
PZ8 .3.W4125 If 2004
[E]—dc21   2002011459
0614 SCP

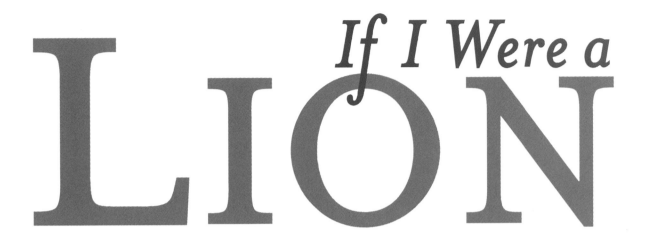

If I Were a LION

Written by *Sarah Weeks*

Illustrated by *Heather M. Solomon*

ATHENEUM BOOKS FOR YOUNG READERS

NEW YORK LONDON TORONTO SYDNEY SINGAPORE

I'm sitting in the time-out chair
because my mother
put me there.
She said,
"You try my
patience, child!
I do not like it
when you're
wild."

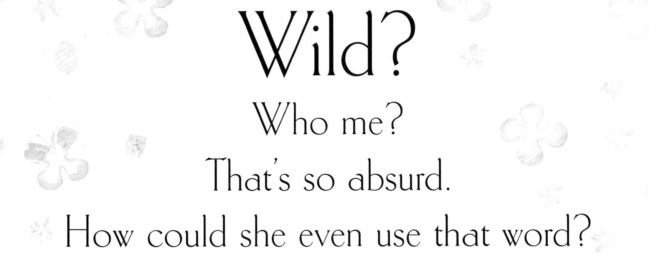

Wild?
Who me?
That's so absurd.
How could she even use that word?

If I were a lion,
I'd growl and roar
and knock the dishes
on the floor.
I'd scare the hair
right off the cat,
but do you see me
doing that?

If I were a bear,
I'd have big claws.
I'd rip up pillows with my paws.
I'd scratch and poke
and pierce and tear,
not sit here nicely in my chair.

Am I howling?
Do I bark?
Rummage through
the trash at dark?

Greet my visitors like this?

No. Not me. I hug and kiss.

Do I snarl?
Do I snap?
Climb a tree to take a nap?
Look at me;
I'm meek and mild,
about a million miles
from wild.

Wild is woolly.

Wild is wet.

Wild's as naughty as you get.

Wild's ferocious.

Wild will bite.

I'm precocious
and polite.

Wild has feathers.

Wild has scales.

Wild has whiskers, tusks, and tails.

Wild is furry.

Wild is strong.

Wild does not know
right from wrong.

Mother doesn't realize
that lions don't apologize.

But when she does,
then she will see,
the opposite of wild is . . .

. . . me.